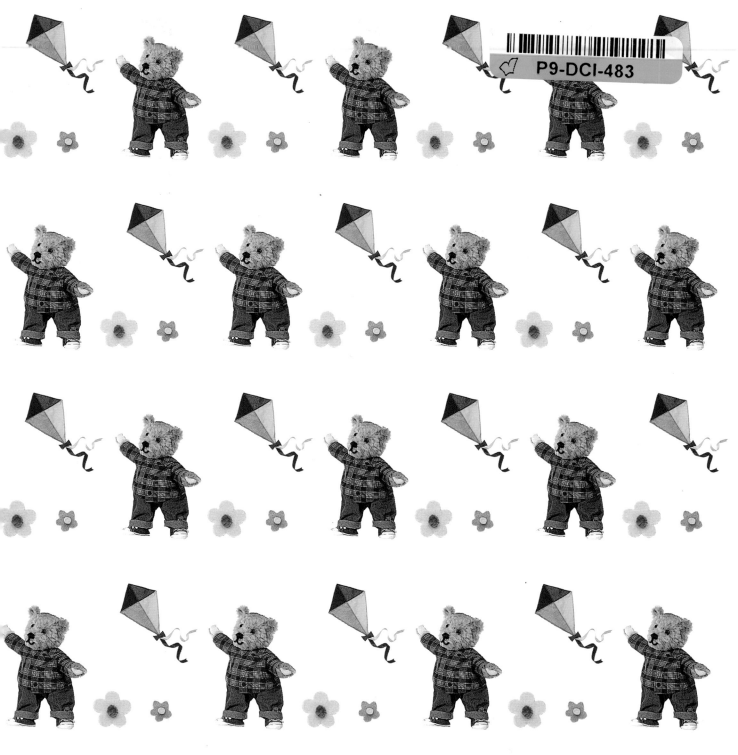

A DK Publishing Book

Senior Designer Claire Jones
Senior Editor Caryn Jenner
Editor Fiona Munro
US Editor Kristin Ward
Production Katy Holmes
Photography Dave King

First American Edition, 1997
4 6 8 10 9 7 5 3

Published in the United States by
DK Publishing, Inc.
95 Madison Avenue
New York, New York 10016

Visit us on the World Wide Web at: http://www.dk.com

A catalog record is available from the Library of Congress.

ISBN 0-7894-1411-2

Reproduced in Italy by G.R.B. Graphica, Verona
Printed and bound in Italy by L.E.G.O.

Acknowledgments
DK would like the thank the following manufacturers
for permission to photograph copyright material:
The Manhattan Toy Company for "Antique Rabbit"
Brio, Ltd. for the toy ducks

DK would also like to thank
Vera Jones, Robert Fraser and Dave King
for their help with props and set design.

Can you find
the little bear
in each scene?

P.B. BEAR

Fly-Away Kite

Lee Davis

It was a clear spring day. P.B. Bear packed
a picnic and went to meet his friend Russell.
Across a field he went, then along the
bank of a stream to the bridge.
"Hello, Delilah," he called.
"Quack, quack," said Delilah the duck.
"Look at my new ducklings!"
P.B. Bear counted 1, 2, 3 ducklings
behind Delilah.

P.B. saw Russell on the other side of the stream.
He ran across the bridge to meet his friend.
"Look what I brought," said Russell.
"It's perfect weather to fly a kite."
P.B. looked at the kite.
It had four colorful triangles,
one red tail,
one yellow tail,
and a big blue bow.
"But I don't know how to fly a kite," said P.B.
Russell started to unroll the string.
"I'll show you," he said.

P.B. Bear watched as Russell ran across
the field, holding tight to the string.
The kite bounced along the ground
until SUDDENLY
a helpful breeze blew it
up, up, up into the air.

"It's flying!"
shouted P.B.
"The kite is flying!"

"It's your turn now," said Russell.
P.B. held the string carefully
and ran as fast as he could.

The kite fluttered
and floated into the sky
above the stream.
Higher and higher it went.
Delilah and her ducklings looked up at the kite.
"Quack, quack!" they cheered.

P.B. Bear ran and ran.
The faster he ran, the higher the kite flew!
P.B. thought so hard about running
that he forgot to hold on to the string.
The kite dipped and dived and drifted
lower and lower out of the sky.

"Quack! Look out, ducklings!" called Delilah
as the kite fell into the stream with a SPLASH!

P.B. and Russell ran onto the bridge.
Together, they peered down at the stream.
The kite was floating in the water, just out of reach.
"Oh, Russell," said P.B. sadly. "I'm sorry."

Delilah picked up
the kite in her beak.
The first duckling picked up the red kite tail,
the second duckling picked up the yellow kite tail,
and the third duckling picked up the string.
They all swam to the bridge.
"You've saved the kite!" said P.B. Bear. "Thank you."
"Quack, quack!" replied Delilah and her ducklings.

P.B. Bear shared the picnic with his friends.
"The kite's not damaged at all," said Russell.
"It will quickly dry out in the sun, and then
you can try again."
"I won't let go of the string next time,"
        P.B. Bear promised.
          Russell took a bite of his pie.
        "Mmm, P.B., there is something that you
        can do better than anyone else I know."
"Is there?" said P.B. Bear. "What's that?"
"Pack a picnic lunch!" said Russell.
"Quack, quack!" agreed Delilah and the ducklings.

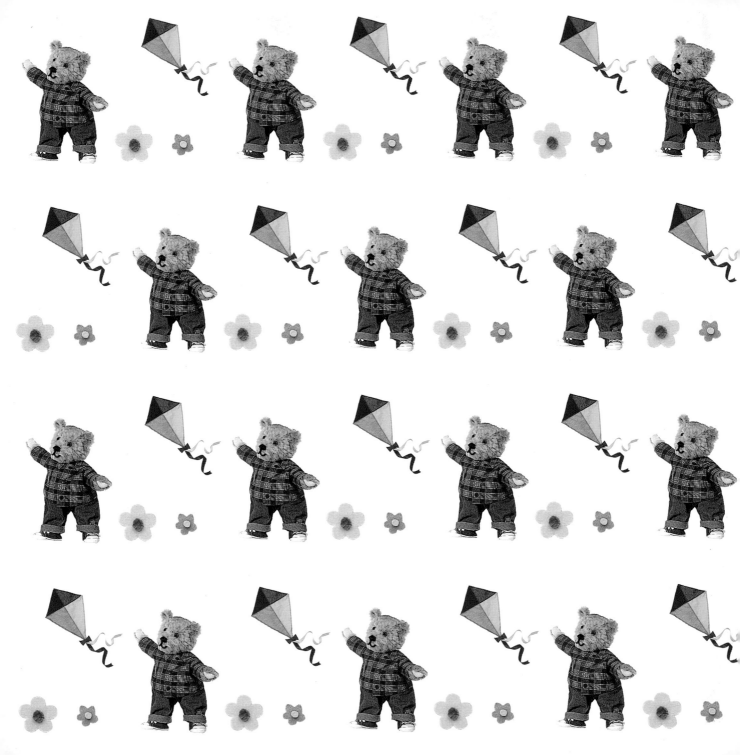